**Northamptonshire
County Council**
Libraries and Information Service

ASHE, S.

Fillet and the mob

Please return or renew this item by the last date shown.
You may renew items (unless they have been requested
by another customer) by telephoning, writing to or calling
in at any library. 100% recycled paper   *BKS 1 (5/95)*

First published in Great Britain 2004
by Egmont Books Ltd
239 Kensington High Street, London W8 6SA
Text copyright © Susan Ashe 2004
Illustrations copyright © Chris Mould 2004
The author and illustrator have asserted their moral rights.
Paperback ISBN 1 4052 1020 6
10 9 8 7 6 5 4 3 2 1
A CIP catalogue record for this title is available from the British Library.
Printed in U.A.E.

FILLET
AND THE
MOB

SUSAN ASHE

ILLUSTRATED BY
CHRIS MOULD

YELLOW Bananas

For Edward
S.A.
For Emily and Charlotte
C.M.

Chapter 1

IN THE BACK bedroom of a shabby house in Huddersfield, a thin little cat stretched her limbs and yawned. Fillet had spent all day trying to sleep in a pool of sunlight that kept moving away from her. Now, famished, she rose and padded down to the kitchen. Her owner had gone on holiday, leaving the neighbours to feed her. But, as they were always arguing about whose turn it was, none of them ever did.

A leap took Fillet out into an alley. There were always scraps to be found behind the tinned-tuna factory halfway across town. But when she got there a gang of yowling strays was raiding the bins. Sadly, Fillet slunk off round the corner, where she spotted a tall door with a large cat flap. To be on the safe side, she slipped through it.

Inside was the grandest room she had ever seen. Before a fire lounged a cat so old his black coat had turned greenish. He opened one eye.

'Who are you?' he growled.

Fillet cowered and whispered her name. Just then, a log on the fire crackled, shooting out sparks that lit up the room. The huge cat stared at Fillet and blinked.

'I didn't mean to wake you up,' Fillet mumbled. 'You must be very important to live in such a grand house.'

'Of course I am, my dear. I am a marmaduke.'

'A marmaduke?'

'Years ago, we marmadukes owned the great city of Rome. But hordes of Tourists invaded our homes, so I moved to this country and settled in a town called Pontefract.'

'I was born in Pontefract,' Fillet stammered. 'In a fish-and-chip shop. That's why I'm named Fillet.'

'Don't interrupt,' the marmaduke scolded. 'Now where was I? Ah, yes. One night, a beautiful lady-cat came to the door of my palace. Beatrice her name  was, and she had a coffee-coloured streak down her back. Funny thing, you remind me of her, my dear. Anyway, we fell in love, but one day Beatrice disappeared, taking all our beautiful kittens with her.' Here he gave a long sigh.

'My mother's name was Beatrice, and she was thrown out for stealing a haddock,' said Fillet, growing excited. 'She had a streak down her back like mine!'

'No, no,' the huge cat told her. 'It's impossible.'

Slowly his vast head sank back on to his paws.

'Oh, do wake up!' Fillet cried. 'Couldn't I be one of your long-lost kittens?'

The marmaduke seemed not to hear her. He raised his head and gazed at Fillet with dim old eyes. 'Beatrice!' he sighed. 'My marmaduchess! Is it really you?'

With a shudder of joy, he fell back, stone dead.

Chapter 2

IN TERROR, FILLET fled and didn't stop until she had run out of the town and into a field full of lights and noise. A huge, birdlike winking thing thundered overhead. As Fillet cowered, a delicious smell wafted towards her. It came from a man eating something out of a paper bag at the top of a staircase.

Sniffing, Fillet glided up the steps and found herself in a room full of boxes. A scrap of paper lay on the floor. As she pounced on it, the door clanged shut, leaving her alone in the pitch dark.

A roar almost burst her brain. The room jerked and trembled until Fillet thought the boxes would collapse on top of her. At last, the shaking stopped and the noise turned to a dull throb. But the air became intensely cold. Fillet's eyes closed and her legs went limp. Then she felt nothing more.

Sunshine poured into
the plane's hold, lighting
up a pitiful heap of fur. The
baggage man picked it up.

'What's this?' he said.
'A dead moggy?'

Running down the steps
of the plane, he swung
Fillet over the airfield fence.

All day her bedraggled
body lay in a patch of grass. At
last, warmed by the sun, she stirred.
Groggily, Fillet sat up.

Nearby sprawled two odd-looking
cats. One, a small tortoiseshell with a stumpy
tail, inched closer. 'Where you from?' he asked
Fillet. 'Whatsa you name?'

The second cat, a
piebald female who
had a torn ear,
sneered, 'Eh, Tozzo,
this notta mob cat.
Anyone can see that.'

14

Tozzo thrust his rough little face into Fillet's. 'You wanna come with Bianca and me, you talk,' he said.

Fillet couldn't even think, let alone talk. The two cats looked half savage and they spoke in a funny way. Then she remembered the story she had been told by the marmaduke.

Drawing herself up, she said, 'I am the Marmaduchess of Pontefract.'

'You got a funny brown stripe,' Tozzo observed. 'You a real marmawotsit?'

Bianca bustled forward. 'Dumbhead, leave this to me. How you come here to Rome, eh?' she asked Fillet.

Rome? Fillet was astounded. But she waved a paw at a plane that was just taking off. 'In one of those,' she said.

Tozzo looked impressed.

Bianca strutted proudly. 'Maybe this one a lady, like me.'

The tortoiseshell sniggered. 'Sure, Bianca, just like you. Countess of the Roman Sewers.'

With a mighty cuff, Bianca sent Tozzo flying.

'You stick with me,' she told Fillet. 'We go see Maximus. He boss of all cats in Rome.'

And off they scampered, with Fillet trying her best to keep up.

Chapter 3

SOON THE THREE cats
were trotting down a
maze of narrow streets.
They stopped at a door,
and Tozzo crept inside.

There came a crash
and a yowl, and Tozzo
shot out with a salmon
in his mouth. Behind
him lumbered a fat
cook, waving a
fish slice.

Bianca hurtled after
Tozzo, Fillet scrambling
behind. They flew down
alleyways and over walls
and at last on to a roof,
where they all fell on the
stolen fish. Panting, the
cook shrugged his
shoulders and
waddled off.

Away the cats streaked, until they reached a vast dark space where tall arches reared up into the night. Wild smells came from all around. The three stopped and looked at one another.

'What we do with Marmaduchess now?' Tozzo asked. 'Old Maximus mighta tink she one of Scipio's mob.'

'You dumbo,' cried Bianca. 'Gotta nuttin in you head but dat Scipio?'

Tozzo growled and slinked off.

Bianca turned to Fillet. 'This here is the Forum, babe. Maxie's hideout. Long time ago, Scipio is boss. But Scipio all washed up, so Maximus take the Forum away from him. Scipio *very* mad. He senda his mob to get the Forum back, give Maxie all kinda grief.'

'What if Maximus doesn't like me?' Fillet asked nervously.

Bianca waved this aside. 'You tell Maxie you the Marmaduchessa of Somesing-or-other. He love a bit of class.'

Soon Fillet was following
Bianca over piles of ruins.
Cats were everywhere.
Some crouched in crevices,
others clung to pinnacles.
'Out of my way, trash,'
Bianca ordered.

'Hey, guys, who's
the new lady?' a husky voice
whined down from a pillar.

'Don Maximus,' Bianca
called. 'This lady coming
all the way from Pontefracto
to see you. Is *vairy* big
marmaduchessa.'

A handsome black cat
sprang to the ground.

'So, madam,' he drawled. 'You know who I am?'

Remembering that she was meant to be a cat of importance, Fillet stuttered, 'All cats know about the Boss of Rome, sir. Honoured to meet you, don Maximus.'

'May I ask what brings you here?'

'I came on a visit,' Fillet answered boldly.

The black cat stroked his whiskers. 'In that case, madam, I would be enchanted to show you round my estate. Perhaps in the cool of the evening we could do a little hunting?'

Fillet purred. She had never before been treated so grandly. Maximus beckoned to an elderly tabby. 'Kick your lazy sisters outta bed and give their den to the dame,' he hissed.

It took a lot of spitting and scratching for Tozzo and the tabby to get rid of the sisters, but at last Fillet was installed.

'Phew!' Tozzo breathed. 'You OK, Marmaduchessa?'

'Yes, thanks to you,' Fillet said. 'But when is the food put out?'

Tozzo looked horrified. 'You don't wanna eat no food put out here. Is rat poison.'

'Rats?' Fillet asked in horror.

'Plenty rats. We hunt. You like?'

'But I can't bear rats. And I don't know how to hunt.'

Fillet was in tears. 'What am I going to do when Maximus comes to take me hunting?'

Before Tozzo could reply, Maximus sauntered up, flanked by his big henchcats. Telling Fillet to follow him, he sprang into some bushes and emerged smacking his lips. Didn't she fancy a tasty morsel? he wanted to know.

Remembering to be a marmaduchess, Fillet simpered, '*So* kind. But I am not quite myself yet. *Such* a tiring trip.'

At once the boss began to bawl orders. Cats ran about, and hairy titbits appeared at Fillet's feet. Not daring to say she would have preferred tinned pilchards, Fillet munched her way through everything.

Maximus seemed delighted. Politely he asked her first name.

'Fillet,' the little cat whispered, certain that now he'd know she was a fake.

But Maximus twitched an ear. 'Violet?' he said. 'Violetta, in my language. How charming!'

Fillet was dumbstruck. Violetta! How grand it sounded.

Chapter 4

THE LITTLE CAT was soon enjoying her new life in the Forum. All day she and the other cats snoozed, spitting or hissing at any Tourists who came near. At dusk, Maximus's bodyguard brought food and then Maximus himself would swagger up and invite Fillet for an evening stroll.

One day, as he was explaining to her that he was the greatest boss who ever lived, five or six skinny cats suddenly shot out of a thicket.

'Scipio for boss!' they screeched. 'Yah, yah!'

Snarling to his henchcats to deal with the intruders, Maximus guided Fillet away.

'This Scipio couldn't take the Forum from you, could he?' Fillet asked.

Maximus's eyes blazed. 'Who tell you about that lowlife, eh?' he thundered, and off he stalked.

Fillet cowered. Then she felt a nudge.

'Let's go,' Bianca whispered. As they trotted away, Bianca told Fillet that Maximus could not bear even to hear Scipio's name. The last cat to have uttered it had ended up as fish food.

For some time after that, Fillet kept clear of Maximus. Bianca tried to teach her to hunt, while Tozzo came and went, looking battered and bringing news of ambushes on Scipio's mob. Then one day Maximus sent one of his henchcats round with a special titbit for Fillet.

'It's very kind, but—' Fillet started to say.

Bianca pushed her aside. 'You tell Boss that Marmaduchess vairy happy,' she told the henchcat. When he had gone, she said to Fillet, 'Maxie get mad if you no taka his present.'

A few days later, a man pinned up a poster. It said:

Fillet shuddered. She was terrified of rats and she still could not hunt. As she was trailing back to her den, having again failed to catch anything, a voice whispered, 'Psst, Violetta.'

A straggly tabby stood
there. He said that Maximus
had sent him to find Fillet
the best dinner ever. He led
her down a hole and
through a long passageway.
There was a horrible stench
of rats. But soon a chink of
light shone above them.
With a crafty look the tabby
told Fillet to jump out.

She found herself alone in a busy marketplace surrounded by tall buildings. Men were setting up stalls of fruit and vegetables. Succulent smells arose. Someone threw Fillet a sardine. Thinking this was the promised dinner, she pounced.

Moments later she was surrounded. A group
of strange cats had appeared from nowhere.
They dragged her before a huge
brown tabby.

'So you are the Marmaduchessa,' the big cat
leered. 'Well, I'm Scipio. When your Maxie
comes looking for you, we fix him good. Then
I get to be boss of Rome.'

Fillet nearly fainted with fright but she spoke
out boldly. 'You'll never catch Maximus. He's a
better boss than you any day.'

Scipio gave a furious growl. 'I fix you!'
he bawled.

Fillet was hustled into a cage, and Scipio
ordered two of his cruellest cats to guard her.
Then he swaggered off, followed by
his yowling mob.

Chapter 5

ALL DAY THE sun shone down on to the cage where the little prisoner lay gasping. As evening fell she opened her eyes to take one last look at Rome and spotted a scruffy cat on a balcony. Tozzo!

He pranced along the balcony railing. 'Haw, haw!' he taunted. 'Scipio needs two stooges to take care of one leetle dead rat?'

The guards growled and swished their tails.
Then they leapt at Tozzo, tearing him down
and knocking him cold. A minute later, Tozzo
lay still and silent in the cage with Fillet.

'Oh, dear,' she moaned. 'Poor Tozzo's dead,
and it's all my fault.'

Her stubby-tailed friend opened one eye and
winked. 'Tozzo just resting,' he whispered.
'You wait. Gonna
be best scrap
ever.' He chuckled.
'Old Maximus
itching to fight
that Scipio
and save
his Violetta.'

Back in the marketplace, Scipio's mob had gathered in a mass. At the same time, leaping unseen from gutter to gutter, lurking behind chimney pots, the gang from the Forum advanced.

All at once the moon rose and flooded the
roofs with silver light. Scipio's army gasped.
The skyline bristled with cats. Maximus, the
Boss of Rome, strode out on to a roof.

'Scipio, you're finished,' he called. 'Come out
where I can see you.'

There was a movement in the square. 'I'm right here, Maximus,' Scipio sang cheerfully. 'Take your mangy crew of lizard-eaters and hit the road to Naples.'

'You take your garbage-crunchers back to the sewers,' Maximus crowed, 'and mebbe me and my guys won't feed you to the cockroaches.'

Scipio hissed. He glanced
up. But the moon had slipped
behind a cloud, and the place
where Maximus had stood
was empty.

'I no lika dis. Where they
all gone, boss?' one of Scipio's
mob muttered.

A tremendous screech split
the air. Every corner of the
square seethed with brawling
cats. Windows flew open,
basins of water came
sloshing down.

In the cage, Tozzo perked up. 'Big fireworks in the marketplace,' he told Fillet. 'Maxie's here.'

With that, Tozzo braced his muscles and bent one of the bars. 'I better go and help. First I take you back to the Forum.'

Fillet plucked up her courage. 'No,' she said. 'I can get there on my own.'

Minutes later, she stood at the edge of the deserted Forum. An ominous stench hung in the air. The little cat shivered. Rats! She could hear them scampering along the ditches. Her brain raced. The rats have come to steal the Forum, she thought. I've got to warn Maximus.

In the square, the rival gangs stood back panting while Maximus and Scipio circled each other warily.

Scipio lashed out. Maximus dodged. He went for Scipio's throat but had to leap clear as the powerful tabby lunged with his hind legs. The two cats backed off, snarling.

Just then, Fillet rushed into the square. 'Rats!'
she shouted, leaping up on to a fountain where
everyone could see her. 'Rats in the Forum!
Come quick, all of you!'

The rival bosses paused and looked at each
other. 'To the Forum!' they bellowed as one.

When the two gangs reached the Forum,
they saw that the ruins seethed with scurrying
figures. Every ditch quaked and brimmed
with rats.

Maximus led a small band to the top of some steps, while Scipio circled with his mob to attack from the rear.

Then Maximus threw back his head. 'EEEEEYOW!' he yelled.

Down the steps his band tore, straight into the rat army. A huge beast loomed in front of Fillet; she went for it, teeth bared. Side by side with Bianca, Tozzo seized the next rat by the tail and swung it round, clearing swathes of other vermin. Then Maximus went down under an advance of monstrous sewer rats.

'CHARGE!' roared Scipio.

'Death to the rats!' echoed the mob.

Scipio's gang poured in. Slowly the rat horde fell back. As their ranks broke and they streaked into the undergrowth, the cheering cats gave chase.

Chapter 6

THE NEXT MORNING, Giovanni, the Forum inspector, and Umberto, his assistant, came to begin the de-ratting operation.

'Umberto, you've started already,' said Giovanni, staring round at the heaps of dead rats that littered the ancient stones.

'Who me?' Umberto poked a corpse with the toe of his shoe. 'These rats been in quite a fight.'

Some time later, the two men came upon Maximus and Scipio lounging side by side in the sun, licking the bites that covered them.

'Eh, it's Numero Uno and the Capo,' Giovanni said, reaching out a cautious hand to stroke the two tattered heads. 'Big night, eh, fellahs?'

Darkness fell. Fillet woke
to find herself piled in a
ragtag heap with several cats.
Bianca's other ear was torn, so
that she now looked even odder
– but after the way she had fought no one
even noticed.

Another cat stirred.
'Eh, Tozzo,' he said.
'What happen? You
got no tail at all.'

Tozzo bent himself in
a circle.

'Whatta you know! Is gone,' he squeaked.

One of the henchcats, looking the worse
for wear but full of high spirits, loped up to
say that all cats except Violetta must come
with him.

Fillet was wondering what she'd done
wrong, when her name was called. As she
stepped forward, hundreds of cats sprang
from the shadows.

'Long live our Violetta!' they cried.

Head in the air, tail erect, her creamy fur gleaming in the moonlight, Fillet trotted between the ranks of cheering cats.

From his pillar, where he stood looking handsomer than ever, Maximus spoke. 'Violetta, as your reward for saving our home from the rats, I am to be your Marmaduca.'

Before Fillet could reply, Maximus turned to Scipio and told him he could have the Forum, since Maximus and Violetta were moving to the much grander Colosseum.

Maximus then turned to Fillet. 'Violetta,' he hissed. 'You deaf or sometin? You wanna be my Marmaduchessa, no?'

'You're very kind,' Fillet said, 'but I'm just a cat from a fish-and-chip shop, and this is what *I'd* like.'

4

Then she told them of her plan. She wanted to move to Rome's old market square. With all the wonderful food stalls it was just the place to bring up kittens. Bianca and Tozzo were always welcome, she said, and Maximus could visit her from time to time so long as he promised not to bring his gang.

As for her, from now on she did not want to be a marmaduchess but just Violetta. After all, she went on to say, that was the name she'd made for herself.